For my sister, Lucy Nokes

The story so far...

ROY RACE IS sixteen, brilliant at football –
and newly signed as a professional footballer
for his local club, Melchester Rovers.

It hasn't been easy, though.

First, Roy missed out on being scouted
for Rovers, as he was at home caring for his
disabled dad.

However, with a little encouragement
from his dad, he gatecrashed the Melchester
Rovers trials anyway, and played well enough
to convince youth coach Johnny Dexter to
sign him up for the team.

Then, disaster struck: Rovers – currently
at the bottom of League Two and with no
money in the bank – were forced to sell all
their players. Just like that, Roy and the rest
of the youth squad were the first team, and
playing in the real football league!

Incredibly, the youngsters made the third round of the FA Cup, where they faced local rivals Tynecaster – a team with billions in the bank, superstars on the pitch, and Roy's hero Hugo up front!

Rovers played brilliantly in the cup game, with Roy scoring an incredible goal... but it wasn't enough. Rovers lost, but they proved they were good enough to come close to beating the best team in the world.

And suddenly, everyone knows the name Roy Race, and what he's capable of...

THE SECOND HE heard the final whistle Roy Race slumped to the ground and closed his eyes.

He had nothing left.

All of the adrenaline and effort he had put into ninety minutes of FA Cup third round football was spent. Above the sound of the blood thumping through his brain, Roy could hear the noise of the home crowd cheering and chanting a name.

'HUGO! HUGO! HUGO!'

Tynecaster United's goal machine, Hugo, the most expensive footballer in the world, had scored the winning goal with the last kick of the game, consigning Roy and his Melchester Rovers teammates to defeat.

How, Roy wondered, would it feel to have scored the winner himself?

He had been so close.

It could have happened.

It *should* have happened.

There had been a minute to go, the score one-all. Melchester Rovers, from lowly League Two, had given it everything. Roy had scored his team's goal, a spectacular left foot volley. But they needed another to win.

Tynecaster had conceded possession. Now a long ball from the Melchester keeper Gordon Stewart was arching through the evening sky. It bounced hard, spinning freakishly over the head of the Tynecaster and England centre back James Campbell to land at the feet of Roy Race.

Roy was onto it, a flash of short blond hair, using all of his outrageous sixteen-year-old pace to beat the panic-striker defender.

First touch to take Campbell out of the game.

Second touch to control the ball.

Then Roy hit it. But, not before he'd begun to lose his balance. Stumbling to the ground he watched the ball cannon off the foot of the post and bounce to the feet of another Tynecaster defender.

The rest was history.

The rest would be read about on the backs of millions of newspapers and watched on a billion electronic devices around the world.

Campbell taking the ball out of the Tynecaster penalty area and into the Melchester Rovers half. The pass to the feet of Hugo. And Hugo's devastating goal that snuffed out what would have been one of the biggest cup shocks in football history.

Roy shuddered, still on the ground, eyes screwed tight. *What if?* he thought. *What if* I'd scored and not hit the post? *What if* we'd won 2-1? *What if…*

'The striker for Melchester Rovers?'

Someone was standing next to Roy. He opened his eyes and looked up.

'Swap?' the man asked, standing over Roy, holding out a Tynecaster United shirt.

It was Hugo. Medium height, short dark hair, muscular.

'I would like to own the shirt of the man who scored that goal,' the world's most expensive player said.

Roy stood up. Overwhelmed, he automatically pulled off his shirt, still hearing the man's name being chanted.

HUGO! HUGO! HUGO!

Then Roy remembered his dad. Danny Race, who was never out of a Rovers shirt, and too ill to watch Roy make his full debut. This shirt was for his dad.

'Uh... no offence,' Roy said. 'I'm going to get this framed for my dad. Thank you, though.'

Roy felt terrible, turning down his footballing hero.

'I understand,' Hugo said, putting a thumb up, smiling broadly. 'I will see you again, Roy Race. Be lucky.'

Roy was stunned. Had that really just happened? Hugo knowing his name. Hugo asking him for his shirt because of the goal he'd scored. What weird world was he living in for that to happen? And to him?

'Oi! Race! All of you! Over here. Now.'

Roy turned to see the colossal figure of the Rovers first team coach, Johnny Dexter, herding the Melchester Rovers players to the far end of the pitch, where one stand was full of fans wearing red and yellow, the rest of the stadium deserted. Roy grinned as a wave of noise from the Rovers fans hit him. Applause. Chanting. Whistling.

'I'm an idiot,' Roy said to himself. 'This isn't about me: it's about Melchester Rovers, the club, the fans...'

Roy jogged with the other players, Johnny Dexter and the club manager, Kevin 'Mighty' Mouse, down to where the Rovers faithful packed out the away end, and were doing their best to drown out the sound of Hugo's name – which was somehow still being chanted.

'HUGO. HUGO. HUGO.'

Lofty Peak, Melchester's giant central defender, put his arm round Roy as they walked to thank the away fans.

'It's recorded,' Lofty told Roy.

'What?'

'All that Hugo-Hugo-Hugo. Look, there's no Tynecaster fans left in the ground. That noise: it's coming from the speakers.'

Roy stared around himself and knew that Lofty was right. Dozens of speakers were booming out the name of Hugo, even though all the Tynecaster supporters were in the car park or already on the ring road home.

Roy couldn't stop himself laughing as he and his team mates went to shake the hands of some of the fans who'd come to support them. He felt good. He knew that – even though they had lost today – he and his Melchester Rovers teammates were at the start of a very exciting journey.

'YOU DIDN'T NEED to give me a lift home, Coach,' Roy said, looking up from his phone as the battered old Melchester Rovers minibus laboured up the steep hill lined with small terraced houses. 'I could have walked.'

'I did have to, actually,' said Johnny Dexter, frowning. 'We don't want you walking the streets tonight. I wanted to warn you first.'

'Warn me? About what?'

'Fame, lad.'

Roy scratched his head. 'Eh?'

Johnny Dexter took a deep breath, then explained.

'This afternoon you scored a remarkable goal against the best team in Europe. Football fans in two hundred countries saw you having a chat with Hugo. Everyone in Melchester knows your name now. That means you're famous. A famous young footballer. That means things are about to be very different. Some people will want to get close to you. If you carry on gawping at your phone like that, seeing what people are saying about you, you won't last long, lad. Social media is a cruel world.'

'How did you know I was…'

'I know, Race. I know everything. And, seriously, if you want praise and criticism, you'll get all you need from me. That goal will change you. There is no doubt it will change you. Either for the better – or worse. It's up to me to make sure it's for the better. And my first job is to deliver you safely to that woman right there.'

The minibus had stopped. Johnny Dexter was pointing through the passenger window. Roy turned to peer out of the window to see a woman standing on the doorstep, a tea towel slung over her shoulder, her mid-length blonde hair tied back.

'My mum?'

'Your mum,' Dexter cautioned. 'And above and beyond everything I've said about becoming a footballer, your bottom line is to do everything your mum says. You might think you're flying in the next few weeks. She'll be doing her best to keep your feet on the ground. So you listen to her. First, second and third. Understood?'

Roy nodded and grabbed his kitbag and a plastic bag off the floor. 'Thanks for the lift, Coach.'

'No problem. And Race?'

'Coach?'

'Get some sleep, some rest and eat well. And take your mind off that cup tie we just lost. We need to concentrate on the league now. We play Weston Villa on Sunday. If we lose that as well, you might as well hang up your boots.'

ROY TRUDGED SLOWLY to the front gate of his mum and dad's terraced house, legs still stiff from his efforts on the pitch. But, even though Rovers had lost, he was smiling. It was hard to believe what had happened to him recently.

It had been so fast. Passing his trial for the team he and his dad worshipped, Melchester Rovers. Being offered youth terms. The whole first team being released, meaning the youth team became the first team. Including Roy. Then his debut, his first goal, the cup tie on national TV. And scoring in that too, wearing the shirt he and his dad had loved all their lives.

He grasped the plastic bag tighter as his mum hugged him on the doorstep.

'I'm sorry we couldn't be there, love.'

HOME LOOKED SMALLER to Roy that evening. He'd spent the day at Tynecaster's Tayir Stadium where every room was enormous. Even the away dressing rooms had been bigger than all the rooms in Roy's house put together.

Roy allowed himself to be hugged by his mum, then went through to his dad in the front room, wheelchair crammed between the sofa, an armchair and the TV. Dad looked tired and thin like he always did these days, but he was smiling.

Rocky, Roy's fourteen-year-old sister, was on the armchair next to Dad, dark hair to match the dark expression on her face as she stared fiercely at the TV, not acknowledging her brother in the slightest.

Dad raised his right hand to give Roy the thumbs up. Roy went over to him, knelt down and hugged him.

'I got you something.' Roy put the plastic bag on his dad's knee.

Dad used his one good arm to tip the contents of the bag out. Roy's matchday shirt, a number nine on the back.

'Oh my God!' Rocky gagged. 'It stinks. Bag it up. Or bury it. Please.'

Roy heard Mum laugh from the doorway, then saw a smile playing on Dad's mouth. He wasn't sure if it was the shirt that had made Dad smile or Rocky's joke. But it didn't matter. Roy's dad had been ill for months. After an operation that had gone wrong, he was now half-paralysed and unable to speak more than a word or two a week. So any smile on his dad's face was a *real* smile – and that was something to feel happy about.

Dad studied the shirt, looked into Roy's eyes, then held it firmly to his chest.

Roy didn't need his dad's words.

'I'll get it framed...' Roy managed to say before he found he couldn't speak either.

'Come on,' Mum stepped in. 'Dinner's ready. You set the table, Roy.'

Roy noticed Rocky put her feet up over the side of the armchair and sigh.

'Yeah, Roy,' she echoed. 'Set the table.'

'Can't Rocky do it?' Roy complained. 'I've just...'

'You've just what?' Mum snapped. 'Rocky's got a maths exam tomorrow. She needs to have a chilled evening.'

Roy was going to say *I've just played in the FA Cup and scored against the best team in Europe,* but he remembered what Johnny Dexter had said to him in the minibus. He had to do what his mum told him to do. That was the first rule. Even if his sister *was* agitating for a fight.

                    *   *   *

THEY SAT AT the small kitchen table and ate
dinner. Half way into the meal, one sausage
and a bit of mash and peas left on Roy's
plate, Mum asked him to fill the water jug.

Roy did as he was asked and stood up
to go to the sink. When he returned he saw
that half his sausage was missing. He looked
furiously at his sister. She was focussed on
her meal, smirking, spearing peas with her
fork.

Roy turned to his dad. Dad was sniggering.

Mum sighed. 'You three. Please. You
exhaust me. What is it? What now?'

'Rocky's taken half my sausage,' Roy
growled.

'Not true,' Rocky said.

'She did.' Roy heard his voice pitch high.

'Roy. Just calm down,' Mum said. 'You're

so hyper. You need to come back down to earth. Now, who's doing what this week?'

'School maths test Monday. Football training with Sowerby on Tuesday,' Rocky replied.

'Roy?' Mum asked.

'She took half my sausage,' Roy repeated, outraged.

'I took three-fifths of your sausage, actually,' Rocky boasted.

'Your week,' Mum said sternly. 'I want to hear about your week. Not sausage fractions.'

Roy knew he was beaten. And, anyway, he had another battle to fight. 'I... er... tomorrow I might take the day off college,' he said. 'Do a bit of recovery.'

'Haven't you got any classes at college tomorrow, Roy?' Mum asked.

'I have, but...'

'Then college it is,' Mum glanced at Rocky. 'Oh… and please will you take your sister to training at Sowerby on Tuesday.'

'Sure,' Roy said, hoping she'd forget college tomorrow.

Roy knew why Mum wanted him to take his sister. It was Rocky's first time with a new football team. Roy had set Rocky up with a girl from college who was in a girls' team. Ffion, her name was.

During a friendly moment Rocky had told him that she needed him to do the things their dad used to do for her. Like find a football team. Pick her up from places after dark. Stuff like that. So Roy was determined to step in and do what his dad couldn't.

As for Ffion, Roy didn't know her surname. Not yet — but he intended to find out. He remembered the three times he'd spoken to her. Twice at college. Once on the

Moor. Roy smiled, then he looked up from what was left of his sausage, wondering why the room had gone quiet.

He saw his mum and his sister smirking. He glanced across the table at Dad, who shrugged his right shoulder. Roy narrowed his eyes and frowned.

What were they so amused by? Whatever! That wasn't his problem. *His* problem was whether he should do what his mum said and go to college the next day.

Or not.

ROY COULDN'T SLEEP that night. Instead, he lay in the dark grinning. How many nights had he stared at the Melchester poster on his wall and dreamed of playing for Melchester Rovers? Did he ever really think he'd play for them, score for them, live the dream?

Roy ran his fledgling career though his mind.

His first game had been at home to Kingsbay. When he'd come on as a substitute it was 4-0 to the away team. Roy had been up against a giant central defender who was determined that a sixteen-year-old wouldn't even get a touch of the ball during the five minutes he had on the pitch.

The defender had been full of chat. Roy remembered his two best lines.

One was: 'You'll end up in a hospital bed, lad.'

The other: 'Your first and last appearance in the game and you won't even get a touch.'

Roy remembered the defender had motivated him more.

He'd not end up in hospital if it killed him. He'd get a touch too. And – if he had his way – a meaningful touch.

Roy remembered tracking parallel to Vernon Elliot, Melchester's left winger, as he pushed forward. Roy heard his coach bellow at him to get into the box, so he used his speed and skill to spin free of his talkative marker and break into the penalty area. Roy had re-lived the moment of his first goal for Melchester a thousand times since. The way he had fought his way into the box, lunged at the ball, stretching his leg long in front of him to make contact and slide the ball between the keeper's legs.

What a goal!

Scrambling to his feet, he'd raised his arms.

His first game.

His first touch.

His first goal.

Roy's second Melchester game had been against Danefield. He was given twenty minutes on as substitute with the score at 0-0.

More minutes meant more touches of the ball. But Roy was not on as striker this time. He was replacing his exhausted midfielder, Satioshi Nagamatsu. Coach asked him to play deep, to try to win the ball and feed it to Melchester Rovers' forward, Paco Diaz.

Roy tracked back. Won the ball. Intercepted long passes. Blocked short passes. Leapt for headers. He felt more defender than striker — but he had his orders. Mighty Mouse and Johnny Dexter had a masterplan. This was a team game, and Roy was determined to be a team player.

As his second game neared injury time, Roy won the ball, created some space and looked up to see Paco Diaz making a diagonal run on goal from the wing. He knew that he couldn't change the game as immediately as a striker, but he would do his best from the midfield. Roy put his foot on the ball and turned his back to goal, fooling the opposition players into expecting a back pass, before making a sharp turn and flicking the ball up the pitch with a deft chip.

Paco was onto the chase, beating the last defender to the ball and dinking it over the Danefield keeper. Melchester 1-0 Danefield. A first win of the season for the youngest professional football team in Europe.

Roy smiled as he lay in bed. But he knew quite well that one win was only one win. It had been Melchester's only positive result so far. Slim pickings for a squad made up entirely of the Under-18 youth players.

The season so far looked like this:

One win. Seven defeats. Eight if you counted today's cup defeat by Tynecaster.

Out of the cup. Bottom of the league. Ninety-second out of ninety-two teams in the entire football league.

Roy stared at the strip of street light that was coming through the gap at the top of his curtains. And at the team poster on the wall.

As a fan the season so far made him feel gutted, desperate.

But then he got thinking. Gutted was how he felt as a fan. But how did he feel as a player?

Roy sat up.

Determined. That's how he felt. Like he could do something to make Melchester Rovers great again. They'd been great before his dad was ill, back when he followed them home and away. Now Roy didn't just have to sit in the stands and feel happy or sad: now he could do something about the future of the team he and his dad loved. And that would begin with the game next Sunday that Coach had been talking about.

Weston Villa at home.

A must-win game.

MONDAY MORNING, TEN-PAST-EIGHT and Roy was in the front room with his dad watching an FA Cup third round review. His mum had been out cleaning the Halifax Building Society in town since half-five. Weekday mornings meant Roy needed to get his dad up, dressed, fed and settled in the front room for when Mum got home.

'Open the curtains, Roy,' Mum said, bursting into the room. 'The pair of you? Sitting in the dark like that!'

Roy stood up to open the curtains.

'Why are you still in your PJs?' Mum looked surprised.

Roy heard himself putting on the voice he used to speak in to get a day off school while pretending to be ill. 'I didn't sleep a wink, Mum. My muscles are tired too. I think I'll take the day off college.'

'You won't.'

'But Mum...'

'We had a deal.' Mum's voice was clear and calm. 'You sign a week-to-week contract with Melchester. You train with the team in the mornings. And you go to all the classes you can at college. Remember?'

'Yes. But yesterday was a big day,' Roy whined. He desperately wanted to spend the day with his feet up. His legs were heavy, one ankle sore. 'Me and Dad are watching the football.'

Mum sighed. Roy could sense she was

wavering, as Rocky appeared in the doorway, wearing her school uniform.

'But Mum, Roy's on a week-to-week contract,' Rocky warned, staring directly at her brother with a grin. 'You said that if Rovers release Roy, or if he gets injured, he'll have nothing to fall back on. College is still really important for his life chances. I'm worried for him.'

Mum stood up and snapped. 'Keep out of this, Roxanne.' She sighed and put her hand on Roy's shoulder. 'Irritating though your sister is, Roy, she's right. Get dressed. Go to college. Now.'

'But...'

'And stop saying but.'

Roy looked at his mum. He was beaten. He walked slowly to the door, like a footballer being substituted before half time. He flashed Rocky a scowl.

'And, anyway,' Mum said. 'You might see someone you know on the bus.'

'What?' Roy was suspicious. What was she talking about?

He left the room, hearing his sister laughing as he stumbled up the stairs. Did they know about Ffion? How? And what did they think they knew?

FFION WAS NOT on the bus. Roy was disappointed. What better day to see a girl he liked than the morning after he'd scored a goal in the FA Cup on TV? Then again, he wondered whether she'd be that impressed. Roy didn't know her that well, but he imagined she wouldn't like it if he was full of himself.

Although Ffion was not on the bus, there were plenty of other people who knew who

Roy was and what he'd done. Two old women smiled at him as he collected his free newspaper from the front of the bus.

'Well done, Roy of the Rovers,' they said in unison.

Roy said thank you and smiled.

Some boys in school uniforms stared at him, then looked quickly away, one of them hiding a Tynecaster bag as Roy walked past them to the back of the bus.

Roy was aware that other people were watching him too, just like Johnny Dexter had predicted: people knew him now. He found an empty seat, put his head down and turned the newspaper to the back page.

PENNILESS KIDS PUSH MILLIONNAIRES ALL THE WAY!

League Two Melchester so close to shocking city slickers

As the bus accelerated into traffic, the thrum of the engine vibrating beneath him, Roy read the match report about how a team of teenagers had come within a whisker of defeating the most expensive football team on the planet.

Roy frowned reading it. He knew the newspaper match report was about the game

he had played in yesterday. He could see his name there, and that he had scored that goal. But he just couldn't make the connection between the two things. He'd been reading Melchester match reports all his life, but this, today, was weird. Roy Race could be anyone. Except him.

After reading the match report, Roy checked his texts. He'd had dozens, including one from his best mate, Blackie.

Blackie had been in every class in every year at Roy's school, but last year had moved to London with his mum. They'd not seen each other since. But they still stayed in daily contact.

Well done yesterday mate. Can you call me? Need a favour.

Roy would reply to Blackie later: he

wanted to check social media before the bus reached college. He was astonished by what he saw. Since signing for Melchester Rovers his followers had gone up steadily week by week from 243 to 2,600. Now he had 115,079, sending hundreds of messages, not all of them nice. In fact, some of them were horrible.

Roy stared out of the bus and remembered what Johnny Dexter had said. *Don't read social media. And if you do don't take it seriously. Just listen to me. I'll tell you when you're rubbish – and when you've done okay.*

Through the window and on the pavement Roy saw small groups of students pointing at the bus.

Were they pointing at him? He wasn't sure. He felt confused. Even shy.

Roy swallowed and stood up. At home after the match last night and this morning everything had been normal. His mum telling him off. His sister winding him up. But, in reality, the world *was* different now. His life *had* changed. Johnny Dexter was right: his words from last night echoed in Roy's head.

You're famous now. Things are going to be different.

Roy felt a shock of fear. It looked like people outside college were waiting. For him. He didn't like it. But what option did he have other than to get off the bus and go into college?

ROY WALKED THE fifty metres from the bus stop to college. Up the wide concrete staircase as usual, but the normal chatter and shouting ten minutes before classes was missing.

Everyone was staring. At him.

Roy carried on walking, uneasy. He had decided he didn't like this, didn't want it. But what was he supposed to do? Then two lads from his BTEC Sports course were alongside him, and Roy took pats on the back and smiles from either side.

'Nice one, Roy.'

'Well done, mate.'

Roy felt better now he wasn't on his own. But he knew things had changed: he was a young footballer who had to get used to the fact that strangers would stare at him – and even people he knew would look at him differently.

It was quiet in the main corridor with its mezzanine level above and large staircase. Roy scanned faces to see someone he knew.

The first he saw was Sam Bustard.

What would have normally happened when Roy met Sam after Melchester had lost to Tynecaster would be Sam and his mate, Ben, bouncing up to Roy and reminding him of the score. Then they would laugh that Tynecaster had beaten Melchester, and film his reaction, trying to wind him up, putting his reaction on social media. That's what they specialised in. Filming short videos to make people feel bad.

But not today. Sam was on his own, looking as short and stocky and as up-all-night-gaming-pale-skinned as ever. Roy was pleased that Sam's sidekick and cameraman was apparently not at college that day. He eyed Sam directly. Sam looked away first, just as a girl with long black hair and a huge smile thrust a piece of paper in Roy's hand.

Serena 09845 347292

Embarrassed, Roy said thanks, then made his way, head down, to his classroom, the piece of paper screwed up in his hand. As he walked through the door of his classroom, he didn't notice Ffion watching from the mezzanine level above him.

Roy sat in his seat. Shook some hands, smiled thanks to a couple more. Then things started to return to normal. Monday-morning-college-normal.

Except that, at the end of the lecture, Roy's tutor asked for his autograph.

'It's er... for my son,' the tutor said.

THE INCIDENT WITH Sam Bustard took place in the canteen at lunchtime.

The whole Roy Race fame thing had faded after breaktime. People had got used to a League Two U18 footballer being in amongst them. They'd gone back to what they figured were more interesting things like texting and eating chips.

Roy was relieved.

Bustard arrived on his own and sat down opposite Roy.

'Hi Roy,' Bustard said, looking over his shoulder and shifting his chair slightly sideways.

'Hi Sam.'

'Nice goal yesterday, Roy.'

'Thanks Sam.'

'You must have been gutted at the end, Roy.'

Roy shrugged. 'I wish we'd won,' he said honestly. 'But I'm proud of what we did.' Roy put his newspaper in front of Bustard. 'Read this.'

'I already have. We won 2-1. We're through to round four and – let's be honest – we'll win the FA Cup and the three other trophies. I suppose that makes you hate Tynecaster even more, seeing as you are in League Two. Bottom of it, in fact. I mean, not just watching us be better than Melchester from the stands, but now from the pitch too.'

Roy was aware that other people were watching and listening to Sam Bustard's wind-up routine from along the canteen table. Roy wanted to end this. He just couldn't understand why Bustard would do it. Did it make him happy to try to make someone else feel bad?

Roy sighed. 'Just leave it, Sam,' he said. 'Please. We could be friends, you and me, if you left it. I mean... what do you want me to say? That I hate Tynecaster and all its players and fans because I am jealous that you're so much better than Melchester? Is that what you want?'

Sam Bustard stood up and smiled.

'That, Roy, is exactly what I want, ' he said. 'See you.'

Sam Bustard left Roy feeling confused. What had that been about?

AFTER COLLEGE, ROY decided to walk home past Mel Park instead of straight up the hill to where he lived. His mum and sister would be at home, so he wasn't needed to help with Dad. Not until later.

None of the other players would be at Mel Park because it was a rest day after a Sunday fixture. But someone from the coaching staff might, and Roy wanted to say hello and catch up with any news.

The imposing gates in front of the stadium – Melchester Rovers in wrought iron above them – looked good today. Roy felt a shiver of excitement as he passed under them, then through the tunnel and pitch side. Roy had been in Mel Park when it was empty many times before. He loved it during a game, the sensory overload of lights, chanting, the smell of chips and red sauce. But he liked it now, too. Four stands of deserted red and yellow seats. Like an empty stage in a theatre. But it was still Mel Park.

Nobody challenged him as he walked along the side of the pitch. Roy frowned. It was quiet. Too quiet. He had that feeling in his stomach that something was not right. He stood and turned 360 degrees to see if he could see any signs of life.

Nothing.

Roy climbed the steps to the players' lounge, wooden seats either side. If there was anyone in Mel Park they would be up there. He quickly saw that he was right. There were figures in one of the offices. Roy was glad to see there was someone in. He'd say a quick hello, tell them he couldn't keep away, then be off home.

He knocked on the glass and pushed the door open. Inside he saw three men sitting round an oval table in threadbare plastic-coated seats, two facing him, one with his back turned. The TV screen at the end of the room was blank.

Roy heard the end of a sentence in a voice he did not recognise. The man whose face Roy could not see.

'… and if we lose to Weston, well, this club has one foot in the grave.'

Then the two men facing Roy looked up. Johnny Dexter, large and intense. Kevin 'Mighty' Mouse, short, rotund, wearing glasses. Both put their hands over their eyes as Roy opened the door. They frowned when they looked up and saw him.

'Race?' Johnny Dexter asked. 'Is that you?'

'It is, Coach. Just passing. Thought I'd pop in, say hello.'

Roy heard a laugh as the third man swung round on his chair. Roy had never met Barry Cleaver, the owner of Melchester Rovers, until now. He felt a chill ripple through him as they came face to face. The man's eyes reminded him of a shark's.

Cleaver stared without speaking at first, pausing to study Roy for a few seconds.

'Well, if it isn't Roy of the Rovers,' Cleaver said at last. 'We were just this minute talking about you.'

'Er, hello Mr Cleaver.'

'Call me Barry,' Cleaver said. 'Or Meat. That's my nickname.'

Roy said nothing. He wasn't keen to call Cleaver – or anyone – Meat. And he had read a message in the expressions of Dexter and Mouse. Go-away faces.

Cleaver was still laughing as Roy said 'Well… er… I'd better go,' and backed away, closing the door, wishing he'd not come. Back out in the empty stadium, he jogged down the steps to the side of the pitch.

'Race?' a voice behind him called out.

Roy turned to see Johnny Dexter coming after him. He was holding a large envelope.

'I'm sorry for interrupting, Coach. I just... I don't know why I came. But I'm sorry.'

Dexter smiled a tired smile. 'I know why, Race. You couldn't keep away. All your life you've been a fan and wanted to walk into Mel Park every day. Now you can. You're not the first who's done it. You won't be the last. Well, I hope not.' Dexter glanced back up towards the meeting room. 'Just make sure next time it's not on a day that... *man* is in. He is bad news.'

'Yes, Coach.'

Johnny Dexter held the envelope out to Roy.

'And here's some good news, Race,' Johnny Dexter said. 'After that goal you hammered in yesterday, you've been offered your first boot deal. It's all in here. Take it home. Talk to your mum about it. And your dad. Then come back to me. Okay?'

Roy took the envelope.

'What's a boot deal? I mean… what happens?'

'It's simple, Race. You wear Gola boots: Gola give you money. Four figures in this case.'

Roy looked at the amount of money he was to be given on the letter Johnny Dexter showed him. He swallowed. It was a lot.

'Money,' Dexter mused, 'I am sorry to say, is the bottom line in football these days.'

Roy grinned. He couldn't wait to see the look on his mum's face when he showed her the letter.

'Mum?'

Roy called down the narrow hallway as he burst in through the front door, then again up the stairs. 'Mum, Gola have offered me a boot deal!'

Halfway up the stairs, trying not to trip on the stairlift, Roy heard the backroom toilet flush. The council had installed a temporary toilet in their house after his dad was half paralysed. It was so big it took up half of the back room where they used to have dinner on a Sunday. It made a terrible hammering noise when flushing. Everybody hated it. But no one said so. Not even Rocky.

Roy stood outside the back room to make sure Mum had got Dad dressed again after using the toilet.

'What's that, Roy?' a shout came through the closed door.

'It's a letter from Gola,' Roy shouted back. 'It's offering us money if I wear Gola boots for a year. And I get the boots free too.'

Roy knew this would be welcome news. First, because his mum had three jobs; they were skint and needed the money. Second, because she wanted to start a course at university and needed at least £1,000 to make a start. Money they would never normally be able to get. Roy was excited: he wanted to help make his mum's dream come true in the same way his dream was coming true.

'Maybe I'll get more deals like this, Mum. I might be able to help with lots of things. If I get a proper contact at Melchester. You never know what might happen. We might be able to get a better toilet in the back...'

Mum emerged from the back room with her finger over her lips.

Roy stopped talking and watched as Mum pulled Dad's wheelchair backwards out of the room, turned it round in the kitchen doorway, then pushed it towards Roy.

'Hi Dad,' Roy said.

Dad looked tired and grey today, but, as always, he put his thumb up. Roy gave his dad a quick hug then backed further down the hallway, so that Mum could push him into the front room.

'Your dad's feeling a bit grim, so I need you to make a start on tea,' Mum said. 'Peel the potatoes. Put the oven on. There's a quiche I got from Tesco. Put that in.'

Roy nodded and went into the kitchen. Five minutes later Mum joined him. Roy had already peeled the potatoes.

'Get some frozen peas out too,' she said, filling the kettle. 'We need to get on with it. Rocky's upstairs doing her homework. I think she did well in her maths exam.'

'Yes, Mum.'

'Now what's this about boots?'

'I got offered a boot deal.' Roy grinned,

passing his mum the bag of frozen peas, then the letter Johnny Dexter had given him.

Mum held the peas in front of her.

Roy nodded, studying her face.

'That's a lot.'

'Yeah,' Roy said. 'I thought you could do the first bit of that university course with it.'

Mum plugged the kettle in and waited for it to boil.

'Put the potatoes in the pan,' she said quietly.

Roy did as he was told. He wanted to hear what Mum thought of his idea. But she was thinking. She did this. She thought about things first, then spoke or acted once she'd gone over it in her mind.

'And if I get more deals like this,' Roy went on, 'it could pay for the course later. I want you to do it. You said you needed to study… to get a better job… now that Dad's not earning.'

Mum smiled. 'That's very kind of you,' she said. 'But there are no guarantees... You might not get another deal...'

'I'll make sure I do,' Roy enthused. 'If I keep scoring I might get a proper contract and then in a year or two years when I'm eighteen I'll get a full deal and then we can...'

'Roy,' Mum whispered. 'Stop.'

Roy stopped.

'We need to focus on today,' Mum said. 'The boot deal news is great. And it's very good of you to want to give it to me for the university course. We can talk about that as a family. But what we need to do now is put the potatoes on. Then I need you to see if there's any bread on discount at the supermarket that we can put in the freezer. And Blackie's called twice this afternoon. He says he'd been trying to get hold of you on your mobile, but you're not answering. And

Rocky said something about a video with you on it doing the rounds at school? I feel like I'm losing control, so, I'm sorry, love, but I can't cope with anything new in my head.'

'A video?' Roy beamed. 'The goal?'

'What?'

'The video? Is it of the goal?'

'No. Not the goal,' Mum frowned. 'Something about you saying things about Tynecaster. Not good things.' Mum breathed in deeply.

She dried her hands on the tea towel.

'Now, can you keep an eye on the quiche and put the peas in the steamer above the potatoes? I have to answer an email about your dad's care before six or we've got no cover tomorrow.'

'Yes, Mum,' Roy said, as his mum left him alone in the kitchen, the letter about the boot deal on the kitchen table. But Roy wasn't thinking about boots any more. He was thinking about what Rocky had told Mum about a video. What was that?

Roy went to check social media to see what Rocky had been talking about. Several people had sent it to him directly. A video clip had already been viewed 890 times. Roy talking in the canteen at college, his voice clear above the sound of cutlery and crockery.

I hate Tynecaster and all its players and fans because I am jealous that you're so much better than Melchester.

Roy closed his eyes. He felt winded. What had he done? And, before he had a chance to think about what he'd said, he saw a name on his phone.

An incoming call.

JOHNNY DEXTER.

'Er… hello? Coach?'

'Race?'

'Yes. It's me.'

'I know. I'm calling *you*, remember?'

'Yes, Coach.'

'That film?'

'Yes, Coach.'

'Explain.'

Roy had seen the film only seconds before. He was still in shock, unable to explain it to himself, let alone Johnny Dexter.

'I didn't say what it makes out I did, Coach…' Roy spluttered. 'Well, I did. But

71

they took a bit of the beginning and the end and I wasn't actually saying...'

'They took it out of context is how we say that, Race.'

'Yeah. I'm sorry. They took me out of context.'

'That doesn't matter to me, Race. What matters to me is that after you dropped in earlier the Chairman told us why he was so

pleased to see you. He'd seen your film. He loved it. He wants us to mess up. You do know that? He's waiting for a good reason to... Ah, I can't talk about Cleaver's warped plans for Rovers. But you gave him just what he wanted, that's what I'm saying. This film is bad for the club, bad for you and bad for me and Mouse. I warned you about social media, did I not?'

'But...'

'Do you think the Chairman wants us to beat Weston Villa?' Dexter didn't wait for an answer. 'Well, I can tell you, he doesn't. He wants us to lose.'

'But...'

'No, buts, Race. This is serious. It's more than serious. Your goal at the weekend counts for nothing now. You've cancelled it out.'

'But... but.... but it's not my film. I was

just talking and they cut out what I said before and after. I really said...'

'I don't give a wet weekend in West Wales what you really said, Race. This is about the club. Melchester Rovers. You're the club now. You're not just a school boy arguing that your team is better than someone else's team. You were a Melchester Rovers player when you said what you said. You messed that up.'

Roy felt his lungs stop working, feeling like he might suffocate. Had Coach just said what he thought he'd said?

'What?' he gasped. 'I was a Melchester player... Do you mean I'm not anymore?'

'No... no... you still are a Melchester Rovers player, Race. But only just. I have to tell you that Mouse is not a happy bunny. You have brought Melchester Rovers into disrepute. You'll get a club fine of one week's wages.'

'But…'

'I said no buts.'

'But we need…'

'Are you not listening to me? I know you *need*, Race. I know your family is living on the breadline. I know your dad is ill. I know all that. That is why you *need* not to repeat this kind of mistake or you'll never have *wages* from Melchester Rovers ever again and then you'll really be in trouble. That's why you are getting a club fine and not being booted out altogether. It's a lesson. If you learn the lesson you won't lose another week's wages. If you don't learn it then you are indeed out. Is the mechanism of the club fine system clear to you now?'

'Yes, Coach.'

'From now you do not and will not speak about the club if you think anyone could use it against you. You don't say anything about any other club. Yes?'

'Yes.'

'You know those boring interviews with players on *Match of the Day* where intelligent dynamic men say nothing, using the same few words and clichés they use week in week out, the same ones everybody else does?'

'Yes, Coach.'

'You do that now. You are boring now. You are a walking living breathing cliché. You have nothing to say. Apart from Yes Coach, no Coach, yes Mum, no Mum. Understood?'

'Yes, Mum... I mean... Coach.'

Johnny Dexter paused. Roy thought he heard him supress a laugh.

'Good,' Coach went on. 'Now, shut down all your social media accounts. And, when she has a minute for you, I would like you to explain all this to your mum. The film. The fine. Our conversation. So she knows what's going on. Tell her she can call me if she needs me to explain anything.'

'Yes, Coach,' Roy said, dreading having to tell his mum about this too. And wondering what Johnny Dexter had meant about Mr Cleaver wanting them to lose to Villa. Why would he think that? Just what was going on at Melchester Rovers?

Tuesday morning. Mel Park. Training.

Three tracksuits stood surveying the players as they stumbled out of the dressing rooms. Roy knew two of them. Johnny Dexter. Mighty Mouse. The third he did not know: a small muscular woman with sharp intelligent eyes.

Roy and the others stared at the woman, waiting to be told who she was.

'This, gentlemen,' Coach said, 'is Frankie Pepper.'

Coach paused. Roy knew he was waiting for some clever remark from one of the squad. Roy was pleased that none of them made one.

'Frankie is your new physio and warm up coach. Please welcome her.'

Frankie Pepper stepped forward. Roy smiled. Vernon Elliott started clapping, the whole squad joining in to make her feel at home.

'Very good, gents. Very nice,' Coach said. 'Frankie?'

'Thanks for the welcome, lads. Now, three laps of the pitch. Slow. I want you warmed up. No sprinting. No racing. Understand?'

The squad jogged the pitch perimeter three times. Then Frankie Pepper had them on the floor arching their backs. Lying with their arms out. Making V shapes. After fifteen minutes she praised them.

'Not bad. Some of you are pushing too hard. I want your muscles warm and relaxed, not forced. You can do the forcing now. Because you're supple, you're ready to push your muscles hard. What I've done will decrease the chances you tear a muscle. And – I hope – I'll not be seeing many of you in my injury clinic. Certainly not from stretches and tears. I can't say what Weston Villa will do to you, though.'

A nervous laugh passed among the players.

Now Johnny Dexter stepped forward.

One of the big differences about training with a professional team for Roy was drills. After stretching. It was different. It felt almost scientific.

Johnny Dexter put the players in threes.

'Triangles. Five yards apart. Pass the ball, then run in between the other two players. Then again. Keep it going. Fast pace. No slacking. Don't look up. Focus on the ball. The three of you and the ball are a machine. You are one. You're not individuals. You're parts of our machine. This is teamwork. Understood.'

Roy was grouped with Vic Guthrie and Lofty Peak.

They started slowly, then, finding a rhythm, picked up the pace. Pass, run, turn, receive. Then repeat. Out of the corner of his eye, Roy could see other trio's balls going astray, but he and Vic and Lofty were on it. The grass was dry, the ground hard. Roy wondered whether it had been watered. Probably not, he thought. It would cost more money to water the training pitches. He knew how hard up the club was.

'My sister taught me this one,' Vic said, breathless. 'She's doing her FA badges. This is one of her favourites.'

'Shut it, Guthrie!' Johnny Dexter shouted from the touchline. 'No talking. You don't exist. You're just a part of a machine. Understood. You can forget your Cup heroics at Tynecaster. You lost. You're out of the cup. You are bottom of League Two. Now focus. And faster: I want it faster.'

After more sets of drills and running, the players walked off the training pitch and into the dressing rooms in the stadium. Plain plastered walls. Paint peeling off wood. A smell of damp.

'That was hard work,' Lofty grumbled.

Vic shook his head. 'Nah,' he said loudly. 'That wasn't hard work.'

Coach put his head round the corner just as Vic was talking.

'Half an hour. I hope you brought your own sandwiches because the days of three-course meals after training are two divisions away. Then we'll look at a video of the match from the weekend. See what we did wrong.' Johnny Dexter locked eyes with Vic.

'Guthrie?'

'Coach?'

'Not hard enough for you, eh?'

'Er… no, Coach,' Vic grinned.

Johnny Dexter nodded, taking his phone out of his pocket. 'Good. Thank you for that input. I have a call to make.'

The players sat in silence as Johnny Dexter made his call.

'Hello? Lily? How are you? Good. Listen, are you free Friday morning, ten to midday? Yes? Great. I've got some young footballers I want to bring up. Can you help? Great! Okay. We'll be there for ten sharp. And Lily? Mud, yeah? And ice. That sort of thing.'

AFTER LUNCH – SOME players racing over the road to the petrol station to grab a sandwich or pasty – the whole Melchester Rovers team gathered in the video room.

'I've made up a compilation of our defensive highs and lows in the Tynecaster match,' Mighty Mouse, team manager, announced. 'I want you to watch. How did each Tynecaster attack end? Then discuss.'

They watched a series of twenty clips,

where Tynecaster had the ball and were forcing Melchester to defend.

Shoulder to shoulder challenges. Melchester losing most of them, because the Tynecaster players were bigger and stronger.

Great saves from the Melchester keeper, Gordon Stewart.

Melchester backing off, conceding shots on goal that went wide and conceding free kicks too.

Clearances off the line. Notably from Vic and Lofty.

Strong headers away.

Then – Roy noticed – towards the end of the game, tiredness. That was how they'd conceded the last goal. They were shattered.

'I'll tell you what we're good at.' Johnny Dexter stood up. 'What you deserve praise for. Great keeping. Strong in the air. 100% commitment. Strength against much bigger men. And mobility. You have all that. And – for the record – I am immensely proud of you and what you did at Tynecaster.'

Coach paused to let the players enjoy the compliment.

'However, we must move on. We know what we're good at. But what about our weaknesses?' Johnny Dexter asked. 'How can we get better?'

Roy's hand shot up. Vic Guthrie's too.

'Guthrie?'

'We need to commit to tackling sooner. We back off and then concede free kicks in range of Gordon's goal.'

'Stewart? Is Guthrie right?'

'Yes, Coach.'

'What else? Roy?'

'We matched them. For 80 minutes we matched them. But then we fell away. They were fitter. That's why I scuffed my shot at the end: I'm not fit enough. That's why we couldn't catch Hugo at the end.'

'Lads?'

Roy saw most of the other players nodding. They all looked shattered at the memory of it.

The conversation went on. Until Johnny Dexter ended it at 1 p.m.

'That's it lads. Now listen up. Tomorrow, I want you here at half-eight sharp. I've set up a practice game against the Prestwich B team. Their coach is Paul Ntende, an old Rovers player and a mate of mine. They play five-at-the-back hard-man counter-attacking football like Weston Villa. We're going to see if we can find a way of breaking them down. Behind closed doors.'

Roy saw his teammates' eyes light up at the chance of playing a Championship team. There'd be internationals in the line-up. Johnny Dexter nodded to himself as he surveyed their excitement.

'Then a rest day on Friday, boss?' Vic Guthrie said. 'That call you just made? Was that some sort of spa treatment place? Mud packs? Ice baths? That Lily you were talking to? A bit of team building?'

'Yeah, Guthrie. Something like that. A bit of mud and ice.'

'What we doing, Coach?' Paco Diaz asked, sounding nervous.

'You'll see, Diaz. You'll see.' Johnny Dexter picked up his file and left the room, laughing.

Roy wondered what Coach had lined up for them on Friday. He felt shattered mentally and physically. What a day. He hoped he'd have the energy for the rest of the week. And now? Now it was 1 p.m. and Roy was meant to head to college for a 1.30 p.m. class.

Roy stood at the bus stop and saw most of the rest of the team heading over the road to the retail park. To Nandos for a second lunch. He felt left out. And hungry. And cross at his mum.

After ten minutes, the bus that was meant to come didn't. Roy frowned. He was going to be late for college. How stupid was this?

Too stupid, he decided. He'd go home. Find something in the fridge. Put his feet up. Get some rest. Watch TV with his dad. He knew Mum wouldn't be happy. But she wouldn't be back from work until after he'd taken his sister to her training, so how was she going to know he'd not bothered going to college?

Roy crossed the road and headed uphill, home.

AFTER A PLEASANT afternoon recovering in the front room at home, Roy arrived, with his sister, at the council sport centre pitches in town where her new team, Sowerby, trained in the week. A full-size football pitch, fenced off from other sporting pitches. Bright floodlights casting shadows in a dozen directions at once. A G4 all-weather surface underfoot.

Roy saw Ffion wave, then jog over to him, the floodlights behind her dazzling him slightly. She looked taller than the other girls. Her red hair was tied up firmly at the back.

Roy felt his heart begin to beat a lot faster than it should have been from just walking across town.

Then he noticed Rocky studying him.

'What?' he asked sharply.

Rocky grinned as Ffion arrived. 'Oh.. nothing,' she laughed. 'Hi, Ffion.'

'Great to see you, Rocky,' Ffion said. 'Thanks for coming. I thought you could train with the B team today, we'll see how you get on. Is that okay?'

'Great,' Rocky said.

Ffion frowned at Roy. 'You staying?'

'Suppose,' Roy replied.

'You can do me a favour, then?'

'Er… okay.' Roy had been planning to read his copy of the Tynecaster match programme from the weekend. But he stuffed it in his back pocket. He'd read it later.

Ffion explained what she needed. The

regular Sowerby coach had not come in. Again. Ffion was going to coach the A team, but she needed someone to coach the Bs.

'So… er… what do you want me to do?' Roy said, looking at fourteen girls warming up, waiting to be coached.

Ffion smiled. 'Well, because we're girls, I want you to focus mainly on skipping.'

'What?' Roy asked.

'Skipping. Then some yoga.'

'Eh?'

Ffion stared at him. 'I'm joking, Roy. About gender stereotypes and football. You know?'

Roy did not reply. He barely knew what she was talking about and thought it best to keep his mouth shut.

'What would you do at Mel Park?' Ffion smiled.

'Warm up. Short passing drills. Bit of shooting practice for fun at the end.'

'Great,' Ffion said. 'Do that. How about three players in a triangle? Each has to pass to another player, then run between the other two players, to be ready to receive the ball. Fast, then faster. Five yards apart? I think my Bs can cope with that. You've got 45 minutes.'

Roy had never done coaching before. Not even juniors. But the girls were all looking at him like he knew what he was doing. Roy coughed. He knew he was nervous, but he also knew that he needed to do this well. Not for him, but because Rocky was there. This was her first day. If he made a mess of it then she'd be embarrassed. He had to pretend he was confident. He was pleased he'd done the same drills with Melchester Rovers earlier that day. At least he knew what he was talking about.

They started with three laps of the pitch.

Roy ran with them: he'd always liked coaches who did everything they were asking the others to do.

'Slow,' Roy said, remembering what has impressed him about Frankie Pepper's training session earlier that day and what she'd said. 'I don't want you forcing it and injuring yourself.'

Warmed up, Roy made the players do five minutes of stretches. Again he used Frankie Pepper's examples. He felt good. Felt like he was doing what a coach should do.

Next he put the girls in threes. He explained the drill. 'Keep passing and moving. Try to make it faster as you go. See how fast you can do it before it breaks down. Then go again. It's about teamwork. Okay?'

After twenty minutes Roy decided to move on and called out what he wanted to happen next.

'Penalties. Me in goal. Miss and you're out. No rebounds. The last man. I mean, woman... girl.... -standing wins... erm...' Roy went for his back pocket. 'This programme from the Tynecaster versus Melchester match two days ago.'

'Signed?' the tallest of the players asked.

Roy studied the programme. 'Erm... no, it's not. Sorry. It's just the programme.'

'By you?' the girl said. 'Will *you* sign it?'

'Me? Oh... okay... yeah.' Roy was taken by surprise. 'If you like.'

'I like,' the girl said, a smile playing across her lips.

Roy coughed for a second time, then asked the girls to line up for the penalty shoot-out. In the first round, eight of the fourteen players scored, with one left to shoot.

Rocky was last to go. His sister had not spoken to him all session.

Roy's sister spotted the ball, then eyed her brother. Two steps back. Two more, her eyes on Roy all the time, not giving him a clue where she might hit it. Then she was onto it, striking the ball hard and high. Top right corner. Roy had no chance.

Roy brushed himself down. 'Right,' he said. 'Round two.'

Four out of nine scored in the second round. Rocky had gone bottom left. Roy

couldn't get close to that either. Two players scored in round three, including Rocky, who put it bottom right. The A team had finished training now and had come to watch the finale.

Now only the girl who wanted the autograph and Rocky were left in.

The autograph girl stepped up first. Her shot was powerful, but she was unlucky, the ball hitting the post and bouncing back at her. She promptly buried the rebound with a neat volley, then shrugged.

Now it was Rocky versus Roy. Rocky spotted the ball and looked again into Roy's eyes. But Roy had worked her out. She'd gone for three of the corners. If she could put four past her brother, one in each corner, she'd walk home happy. She could wind him up about that for weeks.

Roy stood slightly to the right, inviting

his sister to hit it top left, like he knew she would. But he was ready. All his balance was on right leg and hip, meaning he would be able to leap to the left top corner and reach it.

Roy knew he had this.

Roy watched Rocky step back four paces, breathe in and out, eyes on her brother all the time, then run at the ball. Just as she was about to strike it Roy leaped with all his power to the top left corner, his fingers almost reaching the corner where post and bar met. As he fell back to the ground he looked down him to see the ball rolling slowly over the line at the dead centre of the goal. Then he heard laughing. Both the A and the B team were in stitches.

Roy stayed on his back, eyes shut. *That*, he thought, *was embarrassing*.

'Right everyone.' Roy heard Ffion's voice

and sat up quickly. 'A ten minute game. As v Bs. And I think we'll sub that keeper off. He looks like he could do with a rest.'

Roy was relieved. Now he could sit it out and see if his sister really was as good as he thought she was.

THE AS V BS match was played across the width of the pitch. Tight, with little space to play with. Ffion stood next to Roy and shouted out the rules from the touchline.

'No passes or shots of more than ten yards. Nothing above head height.'

Then the girls got stuck in. With so little space to play with the game was all about short passing and movement off the ball.

'So why aren't you playing?' Roy asked.

Ffion sighed. 'Coach has let us down again. He's been with us – on and off – for eighteen months, but recently he's left us to it. So I have to do it. I don't mind. I've got the badges. Some of them.'

Ffion paced up and down the touchline calling out certain players. Roy stood in one place, watching his sister.

Very quickly Rocky became the hub of the B team. She moved around the middle of the pitch, turning 360 degrees to receive passes, then play the ball out. She was clearly the most effective midfielder on the pitch.

The key moment of the game was when a pass came to Rocky from her defence. She took the ball, backed into her marker, then side footed it to a girl on her left. Next Rocky turned and powered to her right, heading straight to the A team goal. Two passes later the ball was at her feet again, wide on the right. Rocky paused, looked up, then slid a pass in at an angle to the A team goal.

Roy hadn't seen her coming, but the

autograph girl from his coaching session was on the end of the ball, clipping it past the exposed A team keeper.

Roy glanced down the touchline to Ffion to see her reaction to the move. She was clapping, a thoughtful look on her face.

After the game finished, Ffion came over.

'She's good,' Ffion said.

'I know,' Roy replied.

They watched Rocky grab her sports bag, sling it over her shoulder and walk towards them.

'Can I ask her to join us, then?' Ffion asked.

Roy shrugged. 'You'd better ask her.'

'Well played,' Ffion said to Rocky. 'You're a pretty good player.'

'Thanks,' Rocky gasped, still breathless, but grinning, after her efforts on the pitch.

'Look,' Ffion asked. 'Do you fancy being on the bench on Thursday for the A team?'

Roy watched his sister as she stared first at Ffion, then Roy.

'Me?'

Ffion nodded. 'Why not? You're good enough. More than good enough.'

'Sure. I mean... Thanks. Yes. Please.'

Ffion smiled then looked at Roy. 'You can come and watch, if you like.'

'I will,' Roy said.

'You might learn something,' Ffion added.

'I might.'

Rocky and Roy walked home through the city centre, then up the Terrible 200, a flight of 200 steps from the bus station to the Moor close to Roy and Rocky's house. Rocky said she wanted to stretch her legs. She was feeling stiff. A walk, especially up steps, would help her recover.

As they made their way up the Terrible 200, Roy forgot the buzz he'd got from seeing Rocky do so well at football, his mind drifting back to earlier in the day.

'Well done,' he said to his sister, as they slowed down half way up the Terrible 200. 'I bet you're looking forward to Thursday.'

'I bet you are too,' Rocky replied.

'What?'

'Ffion.' Rocky was laughing to herself.

'What about her?' Roy felt a rumble of anger. He knew what his sister was getting at. He knew she was going to tease him. But he just wasn't in the mood.

'Well,' Rocky went on. 'You get to see her. Have a nice little chat. That's the reason you're pleased I'm on her team. And the reason you're coming. You couldn't stop looking at her today.'

Rocky was saying all this in a jokey voice. It was part of their usual sister-brother banter. But Roy didn't feel like laughing. He'd had enough of today. College. The video. Mel Park. Now this.

Roy stopped. Rocky stopped. Then it came pouring out. 'I came today for *you*,' he said. 'I came today because of what you said about Dad not being able to help you with football last week. I did it because I felt sad for you and for Dad and for me, not because I like Ffion, which I do, but that's not the point and that's not why I'm here.'

Roy started climbing the steps again. Rocky followed in silence as they walked up the last of the Terrible 200. At the top Roy felt Rocky's hand on his arm.

'Wait,' she said, her breathing uneven.

They both turned and looked across the city. It was dark now and Melchester looked like a bowl full of stars.

'I'm sorry,' Rocky said. 'It was only a joke.'

'I know,' Roy said. 'I've just had a funny day, Rock. The kind of stuff I need Dad for, but don't want to worry him about. Or Mum.'

'So tell me about it,' she said. 'You've helped me. Maybe I can help you. I do actually like you a bit, you know.'

Roy smiled and the Race children walked over the moor, Roy talking, Rocky listening.

Mum was out when Roy and Rocky got home. She'd nipped down to the supermarket. Roy settled down next to his dad to play a bit of FIFA in the front room. Five minutes later he heard the door open, then Mum hanging her coat up in the narrow hallway.

Normally he would have jumped up and helped her through the door, but Melchester were three-two up in the Champions League semi-final against Bayern Munich and Roy was 100% focussed on taking Rovers to the final.

He loved FIFA time with his dad. Taking

their team from League Two, up the leagues to glory with no thoughts about college, about films making him look stupid, about him missing last minute sitters against Tynecaster to worry him. Just him, his dad and FIFA.

Mum appeared in the front room doorway and dropped a bag out of each hand. Roy glanced from the screen to see her. She looked tired. Very tired. He quickly paused the game. He'd make her a cup of tea.

'Why weren't you at college this afternoon?' Mum sighed.

Roy got to his feet. He half-thought to ask her how she knew. But she knew. That was what this conversation was going to be about and there was no point in avoiding it.

'I was tired after training,' he said. 'They worked us hard again.'

Mum was shaking her head. 'Do you

remember that conversation we had where I said you could sign for Rovers if you carried on at college and you said yes? And how we had it again yesterday and you said yes?'

'Yes,' Roy replied.

Mum didn't speak. Roy looked at his dad. Everyone in the room knew that Mum was speaking in the voice she used when she was seriously unhappy. Calm. Quiet. Worse than shouting.

'Don't look at your dad for help,' Mum said. 'He agrees with me. 100%.'

Roy stood up, felt a rush of blood to his head. He wasn't so sure Dad did agree with her. She could at least hear him out. So he started.

'Mum, I need to focus on the football,' he argued. 'If I'm tired I need to rest. College comes second now. Football brings in boot deals and wages. It could pay for you to go to university if you want it to. We need that more than we need college.'

Silence.

Mum looked at Dad.

Dad looked at Mum.

And Roy frowned. He hated the way his parents could look at each other and seem to hold whole conversations in silence.

Then Mum was talking again.

'You are on a week-to-week contract with a League Two football team that could go out of business any day now. You are one serious injury, or one more stupid social media post, from being kicked out. More likely than not you won't be a professional footballer by the end of the season.'

'What?' Roy shouted.

'It's true,' Mum said, slumping into her armchair. 'We all know you are an exceptional footballer and that you work hard. But there are thousands like you, Roy. Most of them at football clubs that are going to make it to the end of the season. You are not. Your chances are slim.'

'So I have to give it everything. All the more reason to. If I need to rest, Mum, I'm going to rest. Then I have better than a slim chance.'

'No.'

'Yes. Mum, you don't know what you are talking about.'

Mum leaned forward. 'I don't like how you are talking to me. And how you are *not* talking to others: Blackie's mum has been onto me again. You've not replied to your best friend's texts and calls. Is he too insignificant to you now you are a professional footballer?'

'No, I...'

'Have you called him?'

'Well... er... not yet. No, I...'

'You need to think about what matters most,' Mum interrupted.

'I do.'

Roy glanced at Dad. He needed Dad's help. In the past – when he could speak – his dad would stick up for him sometimes, help him argue his corner. Not today. His dad said one or two words a week now. If they were lucky. It made Roy feel all the more depressed and all the more angry with his mum.

'I can go back to college if the football goes wrong.'

'Go back?' Mum gasped. 'So you're leaving now? Is that right?'

'I don't know. No. Maybe.' Roy imagined life away from college. He'd be able to relax more, recover, train better too. All his other team mates did. None of them had to go to college.

'I could look after Dad in the afternoons while I'm recovering from training,' Roy suggested. 'Maybe it's a good idea.'

Mum was on her feet again now. Her eyes were red-rimmed. 'This family is falling apart,' she shouted. 'You really think that giving up college is a good idea. It's education. It's free because you're sixteen. That's what this family is going to do on my watch. Get educated. Look at me. I'm a cleaner. I work in a care home. I earn the minimum wage on a good day. I have to go to the supermarket most days and fight with old ladies for the discounted bread and quiche, even though I hate quiche. If I'd have got an education instead of making stupid decisions when I was your age, like you are, then we might not be struggling to pay the bills every week. You'd be stupid to give that up for a one-in-a-hundred chance of becoming a footballer.'

Roy felt cornered. He wanted his dad to speak.

Roy turned to look at him, desperate at what he had lost with his dad's illness.

'You want me to play for Rovers, don't you Dad? You think it's more important than college. Do you think I'm stupid like mum does? Or am I right? One word. Just give me one word.'

Dad looked at Roy, then at Roy's mum. Then he nodded.

'What does that mean, Dad? I wish you could speak.'

Dad coughed. Mum put her hand on Roy's shoulder to stop him taking the argument any further. But it was too late. Dad opened his mouth, facing Roy.

'Stupid,' he croaked.

And Roy Race ran from the room.

Roy left the house the next morning, without saying goodbye to anyone. His sister was at school, his mum and dad in the front room with an occupational health visitor. Roy didn't want to see them. His eyes felt hot. His muscles rigid. His head was throbbing as he walked down the hill to Mel Park for the friendly against Prestwich Bs.

But he wasn't thinking about the match: he was thinking about his dad.

Dad had called him stupid.

All the happiness Roy had got from becoming a Melchester Rovers player had been wiped away and replaced by misery. This – he had no doubts – was the worst day of his life because now Roy was feeling something he had never felt before. And it was so ugly it made him feel sick.

He was angry with his dad. His half-paralysed wordless dad. He was ashamed to even *think* thoughts like that.

Roy got changed automatically, not joining in the banter with his team mates. Everyone was talking about the team they were up against. A Championship team featuring two internationals. A couple of players who'd been in the Premier League until last season. What if they played well? Maybe Prestwich's coach would be interested in taking them up two divisions. There was a buzz, an excitement. But not Roy: Roy was deep down inside himself.

At one point, Roy caught Coach looking

at him, a quizzical look on his face. Then he was moving everybody on. Time to get out onto the pitch. Time to commit to learning how to beat Weston Villa.

On the side of the pitch, Coach pulled the team into a huddle. To Roy everything felt out of kilter. The row with his dad. The empty stands echoing the player's voices without fans.

Coach started. 'I've asked Prestwich to play like Weston Villa. They'll play defensive. They'll play fast counter-attack. They'll tackle hard. They chat to you and try and throw you off your game. They'll treat you like you're a bunch of kids who don't think you deserve to be on the same pitch as them.' Coach studied his team in silence for a moment. 'I want to stress two things. One, don't rise to their bait. It's a tactic. It's not real. I've asked them to wind you up.

Two, play your way, don't let them dictate the shape of the game. Now, warm up a bit with Frankie.'

As the rest of his team mates warmed up, Coach pulled Roy aside.

'Something's going on with you,' he said. 'I don't know what it is, but if you want to talk after the game, come and see me. But now,' Coach put a hand on each of Roy's shoulders and stared into his eyes. 'Now I need you to focus. The work we do today will determine whether we beat Villa. I need you on the ball. So whatever you are angry about or troubled by, leave it in the dressing room. It'll be there for you when you're finished playing, don't you worry. Football is your ninety-minute escape from that. I need you to just feel the anger and make yourself feel better by playing these Championship players off the park. I want you to shoot on sight. At least ten shots on target from you today. Got it?'

Roy felt a smile spreading across his face, felt a surge of adrenaline in his shoulders and arms. Ninety minutes of escape: he liked the sound of that.

'Yes, Coach.'

'I'M GONNA SMASH your fibula and tibia with one tackle,' the former Wales international growled to Roy, as Roy controlled the ball and played it sideward to Pat Nolan.

Roy felt a shoulder in his back. Something crunched in his spine and he stumbled over.

The Prestwich player put his hand out to help Roy up.

'Ease off, would you?' Roy said. 'This is just a practice game.'

'This is meant to be a practice game for you, right?' the Welshman said.

'Yeah.'

'Think about it from our point of view, kid. We're second team at Prestwich. We impress today and we might be first team. And I've heard there's an agent in the stadium, come to watch one of us. More likely one of us than one of you. So, this is more important to us than it is to you. It's not personal, but I'm going to make your life a misery for the next hour and a half. Understand?'

Roy understood. Rubbing his back, he knew there really was no such thing as a friendly. Everyone had something to prove.

The ball had gone out for a Melchester throw-in half way into the Prestwich half.

He stood with his back to the area and called to Lofty Peak, who was ready to hurl in a long throw.

'Lofty! Yes!'

Lofty spotted Roy and threw the ball to his feet. Roy controlled it, played the ball to Paco Diaz, who lost his marker, then turned and sprinted into the space ahead of them. The ball followed. A perfectly weighted pass.

In a proper game, Roy would never have shot from thirty-plus yards, but he had orders from Coach and, as the ball rolled across him, Roy hit it. Hard. And saw it spin, then thump against the post, then crossbar, the noise of the ricochet echoing round Mel Park.

'Yes, more of that,' Coach's voice boomed. 'All of you.'

The Prestwich players were better than Roy and his team mates. They were fitter. They were cleverer. They had experience.

But the Championship team also had something Roy and his team mates didn't have.

Fear.

They were backing off, over-playing the game, constantly looking over to their coach. Had he seen what they'd done? Would he bump them up to the first team?

The game moved on.

After guessing correctly where the keeper's clearance would land, Roy stopped the ball and played a pass across the width

of the pitch to Vernon Elliot on the far wing. Then he gave it everything. A powerful run, leaving his marker for dead, angling in to the penalty area, Paco Diaz and Pat Nolan flooding the area with him.

The cross came in.

The Championship defence was stretched, shocked by Rovers' bold attacking, and Roy saw the ball skip off Lofty's head, slowing it down, but taking it out of the reach of Diaz, who was shaping his body for a volley. To Roy. Far side of the penalty box.

Roy didn't think about it. He just angled his foot, felt contact and knew that the ball would go over the head of the defender covering him, out of the reach of the leaping keeper, then dipping into the net.

Roy clenched his fists and looked across at Vernon to praise him for his cross, clapping his hands above his head.

'That's the last goal you score,' Roy's defender grinned. 'I'll have that tibia of yours in three pieces before you get another touch.'

But when the final whistle blew, Roy had accumulated twelve shots on target and scored with three of them. And both his tibia and his fibula were still intact.

'SON, YOU RAN rings round us today.'

The Prestwich manager had his arm round Roy as he walked off the pitch.

'Thanks, Mr Ntende.'

'It's good to see a player like you coming through at Mel Park. My God, they need it. If I weren't an ex-Rovers player, I'd...'

Johnny Dexter stood in front of them. 'You'd what, Paul?'

Roy could sense a crackle of rivalry between the two coaches.

'I'd take him, Dexter. I'd take Roy Race to the Championship and multiply his wages by twenty. That's what I'd do. He's a class act. But young, rough round the edges. So you can keep him. For now.'

Roy swallowed.

Coach grabbed Roy by the front of his shirt and pulled him out of Paul Ntende's embrace.

'He's Rovers,' Coach growled, glancing at his rival. 'Roy of the Rovers. And he's going to stay that way.

As Roy jumped on the bus to college, he was wearing a faint grin. He knew Johnny Dexter wanted him. And that felt good.

BACK HOME, AFTER college, Roy headed straight upstairs.

He was confused.

On the one hand he wanted to burst in and tell his dad how the match had gone that morning. That'd he'd had a full ninety minutes and had found his touch and that extra burst of pace he always knew was there.

On the other he didn't want to face his dad again.

He crept upstairs, emptied his college bag out and put his files neatly on the table right next to his bed.

131

Then he waited, lying on his bed, staring at his poster of Melchester Rovers and the other one of an Aston Martin car, the kind James Bond drove in the films Roy watched with his dad.

He knew she'd come.

Five minutes later, Mum came in silently and sat on the bed next to Roy. She had a plate of buttered toast for him. Inside he felt

about eight years old. It was hard to believe he was sixteen and a professional footballer, lying on a flimsy single bed in his box room.

'Can I say something?' Mum asked.

Roy shrugged.

'Things are changing for you fast,' Mum said. '*You're* changing. You're sixteen. It's a hard time. On the one hand you are still a child in your bedroom. On the other the world is opening up for you to do whatever you want. At your age I can't be there all the time to help you make the right decisions. You need to think hard about what you do. It reflects on Melchester Rovers. It reflects on your family. And, most of all, it reflects on *you* and who you are.'

'I did well today. I was back to my best. Someone said there was a top agent in the stadium. I can do it, Mum.'

'I believe you will.'

'No you don't. You want me to do college. You think I'll fail.'

Mum shook her head. 'I said you *might* fail. Most people fail. You just have to have back up. Even famous Rovers players like Noel Baxter and Mervyn Wallace had back up plans. Noel has got a degree from university. Mervyn runs a business and spends hours on it every week as well as football. They've worked hard to make sure they had back-up if the football went wrong. And that was a risk in a way.'

'So why don't you let me take a risk?' Roy said without thinking it through.

'Well,' Mum paused. 'Because you are more than just you. You are one of a family of four. But a family that is in crisis. With your dad being ill and your sister only fourteen, these are challenging times. Think about it in terms of football. Think about teamwork.'

'Eh?'

'*Teamwork*,' Mum repeated. 'We're a team. You. Me. Rocky. Dad. So long as we play for each other we'll survive. If we play as individuals, we'll fall. And until you have a solid deal at a football club that is secure and safe, I need you to go to college. Because everything I said is true. You might be the best young footballer in the world, in the best shape. But Mel Rovers are not in good shape. And what if you did get injured? It could happen in training, it could happen at Mel Park... any player, sixteen or thirty-six, could take a career-ending injury any day of the week.'

'I know. Mum,' Roy said. 'I'm not leaving college. I just felt tired.'

'I understand. And I'm sorry I went off on one, but I'd had a hard day too.'

Roy swallowed. *Might as well get everything out in the open,* he said to himself.

'Mum?' he said. 'I have to tell you about

something else. Coach asked me to talk to you about.' She needed to know about the film and the fine.

DAD LOOKED SHEEPISH when Roy went in to see him after the chat with Mum.

Roy sat next to Dad: he knew he had to speak for both of them. He had to work out what Dad wanted to say and to say it for him – without getting it horribly wrong.

'I'm sorry, Dad. When you said I was being stupid, you were right. I was. I will stay on at college. I'll listen to Mum. She's right. I'm sorry for causing all that trouble.'

Dad nodded his head. But he still looked tired and sad.

'Look,' Roy said, trying not to show how upset he was feeling. 'If I'd said what you said to me, I'd feel bad about it.'

Dad nodded again.

'But you had a point, Dad. I... well, I want to say I am glad you said it. I've taken it on board. So please don't feel bad.'

Dad forced his half smile.

'So, shall we get Melchester into the Champions League final, then?'

Dad put his right thumb up.

'I just need to make a call first.'

His dad looked at him with a puzzled expression on his face.

'Blackie,' Roy said. 'I need to call Blackie.'

ROY TOOK HIS phone up to his room, lay on his bed and dialled his friend.

'Roy?'

'Blackie. How's it going?'

'Good.'

Blackie started talking about Roy's game against Tynecaster, praising him, saying he was proud of him. Then there was a silence.

Roy knew what needed saying to fill it.

'Look,' Roy said. 'I'm sorry I've not called you back. I've been a bit... well... funny for a few days. And I'm sorry. I know you needed my help. And I'm sorry it's late, but what can I do?'

'I've got a trial tomorrow,' Blackie said, his voice quieter.

'Great. Where?'

'Islington.'

'No way,' Roy stood up. 'That's awesome, Black. Premier League. What's going on? Tell me everything.'

Blackie explained. He'd been scouted playing for his college team. They'd asked him to come in for a special day they held every six months for local lads. Blackie finished saying 'I just wanted to know – what with you having had a trial at Mel Rovers – what you think I should focus on. Like, three things.'

Roy nodded to himself and sat on the end of his bed. He was going over his trial. How it'd nearly gone wrong. Trying to work out what he would have done differently.

'Roy?'

'Sorry. I was just thinking about it. Three things. Right. This is what I'd say. Thing one, don't try to too hard. Just play your natural game. Your strengths are your power. And your ability in the air. And you're always in the right place at the right time. You need to show what you can do, but relax or you'll push too hard.'

'Thanks.'

'Thing two.' Roy paused. 'Even though it's a trial and you're in direct competition with the other players there, play like a team player. Islington want you to join their team to play a team game. They don't want some football tekkers-merchant. If you were back at Grimroyd you'd always play me in if you thought I had a better sight of goal. Do that. They'll be looking for that as much as individual skill. Not someone who thinks he's Hugo. It's all about teamwork.'

'Thanks. And three?'

'Imagine your mum's there.'

'What?'

'What I mean is, be respectful and mature. Coaches want to see you respect other people. On the pitch and off it. They look for it as much as ability. Well, almost. Just imagine your mum's there and she wants you to behave. Like you're at your gran's and she wants your gran to see that she's brought you up well. If you mess about and be all cocky, then your mum would be disappointed. Well, it's kind of the same with coaches. Treat everyone right, whoever they are.'

Roy could hear Blackie breathing at the other end of the line.

'Any questions?'

'No, I'm good, thanks, Roy. So how's your dad? How's Rocky?'

Roy and Blackie talked. It felt good. Better than a text conversation or something on social media.

'Rocky's got this game tomorrow,' Roy told his friend. 'It's funny. I can't wait...'

16

Thursday evening.

Parked at the edge of the car park, as close to the touchline as possible, Roy sat in the driving seat of the car, his dad next to him in the passenger seat. This was the first time Dad had been out in Mum's car since his operation. Mum was pitch side talking to other parents. They'd agreed Dad would stay in the car. He was already shattered, so it would save him getting into his wheelchair and tiring himself more.

But Roy could see his sister constantly glancing in their direction from the subs' bench. She had a massive grin on her face. Her dad had come to see her play in a football game! Roy knew that was at least two of her dreams coming true at once. Dad out and about. And playing for a proper team.

With the Sowerby coach not showing up again, Ffion was in charge. Player coach. At

half time, she came over to speak hello to Roy and Dad.

'Hi Roy.'

'Hi Ffion. This is my dad.'

'Hello, Mr Race. I thought I'd come and say hi and let you know that I'm bringing Rocky on for the whole of the second half. We're 1-0 down and losing it in midfield. Rocky can change that. It's nice to meet you, Mr Race.'

Dad smiled at Ffion, then, when she'd gone, winked at Roy.

'What?' Roy asked.

Dad shrugged, still smiling.

Roy turned his attention back to the game. He knew that his sister had been living for this moment all of her life. She loved football. She wanted the same opportunities that Roy had been given. But there were so few girls' teams in town – in any town. And even less women's teams if you did well in a girls' team.

But here she was. In a team. In her town. In her element. This was a chance she had to take. Annoying though she was, Roy felt a strange glow of pride as Rocky took the game by the scruff of its neck.

Ffion put her in front of the back four. Her job: to win the ball and distribute passes to players moving forward.

Rocky's first touch was a tackle, chasing down a Hebden attack and sliding in to clip the ball into touch off her opponent. Then, without stopping, she was back on her feet, moving into space for her second touch, receiving the ball from the quick throw in, turning, then playing Ffion down the wing.

Roy could see the Hebden defence moving deeper, aware of Rocky's threat.

Meaning Rocky now had space.

Her next touch was to take the ball direct from the keeper, control it, turn to run through the Hebden midfield, then play a slide-rule ball to the feet of a teammate.

A perfect pass. The defence dissected. The Sowerby striker one-on-one against the keeper.

1-1.

More players went to congratulate Rocky than the scorer. Roy punched the air.

With ten minutes left, Rocky was tackled high, studs up. She went down hard, her face twisted with pain, making Dad jump forward in his front seat and shout.

'No.'

Roy didn't know whether to be happy or sad. Another word from Dad. That was two in two days. He wondered whether Dad was getting a bit better, before he gave his attention back to his sister, who was on her feet already, standing over the ball, scanning the pitch, not thinking about who had fouled her, or reacting, just getting on with the game.

Roy saw Ffion move at pace down the wing, then watched Rocky hit another beautiful pass to her captain, as she sprinted into the penalty area. Ffion's cross came in

low and fast. Somehow Rocky was onto it, controlling the bounce, drawing the keeper and the last defender, before side-footing the ball into space and the oncoming Sowerby right winger.

2-1. Two assists for Rocky Race.

Roy grinned and felt his dad's right hand grip his left.

And then Rocky was sprinting towards them. Roy could see she was shattered, but beaming. He'd never seen her smile like this.

'Did you see me, Dad?' she gasped.

Dad nodded, his face screwing up.

Roy felt the hot shock of tears in his eyes, seeing his sister like this with their dad. It caught him off guard. He climbed out of the car and walked away, leaving them to have their moment, gazing across the car park. He had a half thought about the mystery training session that Coach had planned for them the next day, then he saw Ffion waiting under a street light and a silver Honda draw up, its exhaust roaring, saw Ffion wave to the driver, then jump in. Then laughter. Roy caught sight of the driver as it came by.

It was Vic Guthrie.

Roy felt like he'd been punched in the stomach.

WINDSCREEN WIPERS LABOURING, the Melchester Rovers minibus drew up in the car park of a small dark church at the foot of a steep hill. Grey clouds were scudding across the sky. In the distance there was a tall stone monument sometimes visible at the top of the pale green hillside, sometimes obscured by squalls of rain or mist. Standing at the entrance to the church was a runner. Small and lean, she was wearing a luminous yellow beanie hat and carrying a small rucksack on her back.

'Oh no,' Vic Guthrie groaned.

'What?' Pat Nolan asked.

'Coach is going to have us run up that hill. We're going fell running.'

Roy tried not to listen to Vic. After seeing him with Ffion the day before, he felt a strange uncontrollable anger towards his team captain. Sometimes Roy wished Vic would talk less. He was always talking, always trying to be the funny one or the hard man. His talking-too-much was part of the reason they were out here today.

'What is this fell running?' Paco Diaz cocked his head to one side.

'Running up hills like that. Then down. Usually in the rain. Lots of ice and mud.'

As the players climbed off the minibus and into the rain, the bleak realisation hit each of them. Vic was right.

Johnny Dexter explained the plan for the morning.

'This,' he said, 'is Lily Halifax. Lily

Halifax is a British fell running champion. That is Stoodley Pike. It is less than three miles away, two hundred and fifty metres high. Lily, here, is going to lead you up to the Pike. Some of you complained that training isn't hard enough. Sadly Melchester Rovers cannot afford state-of-the-art strength equipment and a specialist coach. But we are lucky to have Stoodley Pike and Lily Halifax to make up for that failing. First one to the top wins £20 along with the knowledge that – until we do this again – you are the fittest footballer at this club.'

Roy watched as a curtain of rain swept up the valley. He grinned. He wanted that prize. Then he noticed Vic looking at him. They locked eyes. And Roy knew Vic wanted the prize too. Roy felt an unexpected burst of adrenaline. There was no way he was going to let Vic Guthrie beat him to the top of this hill.

They started slowly, matching Lily's pace in a cluster alongside a drystone wall, the rain seeping in through their clothes. But soon some runners fell back, harassed by the shouts of Johnny Dexter at the rear. Two minutes in the players were stretched out over fifty metres, Roy and Vic already leaving

a gap between themselves and the others on the muddy path that cut like a gash up the side of the hill. This was personal.

Lily Halifax eased up a gear to keep herself ahead of Vic and Roy.

Roy did his best to stay with her. He felt confident. He was good at hills. Part of his fitness regime was to run up and down the Terrible 200. It should pay off for him today.

He was anxious, then, to hear one runner still heavy-breathing behind him. He glanced back to see Vic Guthrie and Roy understood he was in for a fight. He knew he was fitter than Vic, but he was fully aware that Vic had more determination than the rest of the team put together.

As the hill got steeper the surface of the track began to break up into smaller stones, making it easier to turn your ankle. Plus, the track was taking so much water off the hill it

157

had become a stream. They were, in reality, running up a river bed, mud splashing up the backs of their legs. But Roy and Vic pushed on, way ahead of the others now, Lily Halifax just ahead, checking to see where they were over her shoulder. Roy was well aware that she could, at any moment, accelerate and disappear into the mist ahead of them. And he nearly blew it when he fell and cut his knee.

More than half way up now, Roy could feel his legs start to hurt. Lactic acid building up in his thighs and calves. He tried to breathe deeply to get more oxygen into his body, tried not to think about seeing Vic with Ffion last night, but it was eating away at him, affecting his run.

Taking advantage, Vic came gasping past Roy, his mouth hanging open, grunting as he ran. Vic was clearly hurting too, but it was working for him. Roy stayed with him, making him work to stay ahead, waiting for a chance to attack.

Closer to the top. Maybe 300 metres to go and the hill became steeper still. Seeing the run was almost done, Roy attacked. He pumped his arms and legs, trying to do what Vic was doing, giving it his all, taking the pain, feeling the rain driving at his face.

Now he was on Vic's shoulder. 150 to go.

With another push Roy overtook his team captain as the ground levelled out towards Stoodley Pike. A hundred metres, the pair of them were sprinting now, pain and nausea flooding Roy's body.

With 50 metres left Vic picked up his pace to pull level with Roy. Then ahead again.

Roy saw Lily, already at the pike, sipping from a bottle of water, looking back with an amused expression on her face as they hammered at the ground.

Then Roy powered on. Thinking of Vic being number one at everything. Thinking of Ffion getting into Vic's car last night. Instead of the anger slowing him down, he tried to use it to drive him on.

And it worked. They were level now. But Roy knew he needed more, knew Vic would have a final sprint, so Roy pushed again, lunging forward as they approached the monument, both their hands slamming against it, seconds apart.

The two players gasped for air, kneeling, falling to the ground, then both staring at Lily Halifax to tell them who won.

The fell runner smiled at Vic and shook her head. 'Sorry, mate,' she said. 'Blondie here beat you by a leg.'

Roy closed his eyes and tried to breathe deeply.

'You'll never beat me again, Race,' he heard Vic gasp. 'I'll vomit my own intestines up before I come second to you again.' Then he turned his back and started retching.

Once the last stragglers had made it into the lee of the monument – slumping to their knees and gasping for air, some rubbing their legs – Johnny Dexter raised his hand.

As he did, it was like a hole had been torn through the cloud. A patch of blue sky and light appeared. Below them, at the foot of the hill, the players saw the city of Melchester, in a vast bowl surrounded by steep hillside

'Look down the hill to where that patch of green is to the right,' Johnny Dexter said.

The players looked.

'That's the Moor,' Dexter went on. 'Now, follow those threads of hundreds of small brown buildings down the hill. At the foot of the hill is more brown and green. Got it? Yes?

That, boys, is Mel Park. The urban sprawl beyond it is Melchester, city of 250,000 souls. Most of you live there. Most of you were born there. And every single one of you represent that city on the football pitch.'

Johnny Dexter paused and allowed his young team to look at the city before them. Then he began again.

'I wanted you to come up here today to understand that in those houses and factories, driving along those roads, walking their dogs along that canal, there are children and men and women who are desperate for you to get this football team off the bottom of League Two and take it where it belongs. Generations of them. Are we clear?'

'Yes, Coach,' eighteen voices said.

'And I want you to understand that, and take it back down the hill with you and remember it when you train and play.'

Roy looked round at the faces of his team mates. The sun was shining down on them now. The sky had miraculously become blue, the curtain of rain retreating east. A large double rainbow shimmered like a great arch over their heads.

Message received, Roy thought to himself.

When they reached the foot of the hill, Roy felt like something had changed. His teammates looked serious. Every one of them took the time to shake hands with Lily Halifax and thank her. They all stretched out before climbing back into the tight seats of the minibus for the drive back to Mel Park.

Roy was shattered, muddied and bloodied. But he knew what he had to do this afternoon. He put his hand on Johnny Dexter's shoulder.

'Is there any chance you could drop me at the City College on the way past, please, Coach?'

'THIS SUNDAY'S GAME against Weston Villa is the point on which our whole season rests,' Mighty Mouse said.

He'd asked all the players to sit down on the pitch after training. Saturday afternoon. A short training session in the stadium, as opposed to the training pitch. This was where they always trained the day before a game: on the very surface they would be playing on.

'You played like lions against Tynecaster,' Mouse said. 'You nearly beat them. And – love them or loathe them – they're a team

165

of great skill and power, so that was a huge achievement. But I don't want you thinking Weston Villa will be easy. No, Weston Villa are not as good as Tynecaster, but they'll be more dogged, more brutal, more determined. So, in some ways, a harder opponent.

'The game is pivotal because we need to start winning. We need to finish sixth

in League Two this season. Then win the playoffs. That is our target.'

Roy sat with his legs splayed out, hands resting on the grass behind him. He was tired. But not too tired. They'd spent the morning working on pressing, not giving the opposition a moment on the ball, harrying them, tackling, shutting down their space. Some teams hated it. Mouse and Dexter had watched Weston Villa a couple of times and had identified that as a weakness.

'Johnny and I have worked with you on what we believe we need to do. We have picked the team. Each of you knows your role. If you all stick to the plan and play with the ability we know you have, then we'll win tomorrow.'

Like the other players, Roy listened in silence. Every few seconds he caught the eye of a teammate. Lofty Peak. Gordon

Stewart. Even Vic Guthrie. Shared glances passed between each and every player. Roy felt tingles passing down his spine, his heart beating faster. Something was happening to him and his teammates, to Melchester Rovers Football Club. Something good.

Now Johnny Dexter was on his feet.

'We've a press conference at eleven and I need a player to do it with.'

Roy and three others volunteered.

Johnny Dexter stood next to Roy and tapped his football boot with his trainers. He was shaking his head.

'You want to do it, Race?'

Roy nodded. 'Yes, Coach.'

Johnny Dexter grinned and looked at Roy's teammates. 'Roy wants to go on camera and field questions about Melchester Rovers. Good idea, anyone?'

Roy heard the other players laughing.

'Good idea, Race?' Johnny Dexter squatted next to Roy. 'You know the local rag actually asked for you. So did the radio station.'

'Great,' Roy said, knowing he was being used to get a laugh from the squad, but deciding to go along with it. They wanted to take the mick out him? Fine. He could take it. It was all about teamwork, wasn't it?

'Not great, Race. They want you because you're a liability.' Dexter mimicked Roy with a high-pitched voice. '"I hate Tynecaster and all its players and fans?" I don't think so, Race. I'll take Guthrie if you don't mind.'

Roy heard an explosion of laughter behind him. He turned round and grinned at all his teammates, pretended he didn't know what they meant by shrugging.

*　　*　　*

169

AFTER THEY'D SHOWERED and changed, Lofty suggested the players went to Nandos. Again.

Roy declined. 'Thanks Lofty, but I've got to get home and look after my dad.'

He walked home, gazing at an Aston Martin car he'd spotted near Mel Park, which was now overtaking him. His phone buzzed just after he'd put it back in his pocket.

From Blackie.

Good news. Got 2 year deal at Islington. Buzzing. Tx 4 advice.

You really helped. Did what you said. Got in. Boom.

Roy smiled and texted his friend back.

Awesome! You're one hell of a player. Speak soon mate!

And, for the most part, Roy really was thrilled for his friend. After Blackie's mum and dad had split up and he had to move away he'd not been happy. This would make him happy.

Then – mixed into that – Roy had another feeling too. A sort of envy. Wouldn't he like to play in the Premier League? How come Blackie got to play in the Premier League and Roy was in League Two?

But Roy knew it was a stupid thought and he did his best to ignore it.

Sunday morning. Match day. Roy opening the front door, ready to go.

'Do you want a lift in?' Mum asked. 'Rocky can be with your dad.'

'No, it's fine. I'll…'

Roy stopped speaking. He couldn't believe it. The car. The Aston Martin sports car – gleaming red and gold – that he'd seen around town was there. In front of his house.

A short man in a posh suit, balding and smoking a cigar leaning against it. Roy could see at least three people in upstairs windows, curtains pulled back, staring in awe.

'Rod Race. THE Rod Race. Rod of the Rovers?' the man said.

'I'm Roy,' Roy replied, cautious.

'That's what I said, son,' the man said. 'I'm Alan Talbot.'

Alan Talbot waited for Roy to react.

Roy didn't react.

'Yeah, you got it,' the man went on. 'THAT Alan Talbot.'

'That's an Aston Martin!' Roy purred, his eyes on the car, not the man. He'd never heard the name Alan Talbot.

'You like that, do you, son? Yeah, go on then. Have a sit in it. Driver's seat. Heated.'

Roy's first question was why. Why would a man with a posh car offer for Roy to sit in it? It was his mum talking. *Don't take sweets from strangers. Don't get into cars with strangers. Think about why people you've never met want to give you things.*

'Really?' Roy asked.

But the car *was* amazing. He loved it. It was his dream car, the car on a *poster in his room* and he couldn't resist sitting in an Aston Martin. Just for a moment. He was bigger than the man, anyway. He didn't feel threatened. And Mum and Rocky were on the doorstep now. His mum staring hard at Alan Talbot. Alan Talbot staring hard at Rocky.

Roy winced. Now this didn't feel right.

He stepped away from the car and locked eyes with his mum.

'May I ask who you are?' Mum said to the man.

Alan Talbot stepped from the kerb to Roy's front door.

'Alan Talbot, my love. Agent extraordinaire. Representing only the VERY best footballers. Excellence. At all times. And that's why I'm here today. For your son. I'm gonna make him a star…'

Mum put her hand up and shook her head.

'His hard work and dedication will make him a star, Mr Talbot,' she said calmly. '*If* he becomes a star.'

'Absolutely…'

'And he's got a contract already,' Mum went on. 'With Melchester Rovers, thank you.'

Roy and Rocky watched as the football agent stepped back, his voice faltering, whereas Mum just stood her ground, her voice calm and consistent.

'A rolling week-to-week contract,' the agent said. 'In League Two? I take it you did not have representation when you agreed to that?'

'Uh... No,' Mum said. 'But we trust Johnny Dexter. We trust Melchester Rovers.'

The agent rolled his eyes skywards turned to Roy, stepping in between him and his mother.

'Son, I saw what you did against Tynecaster in the FA Cup. That goal. And you almost won it in the last few minutes there. Playing against Galacticos!'

Roy looked at Mum. He heard the words she had used two days before as clear as a bell.

You're sixteen and I can't be there all the time to help you make the right decisions. You need to think hard about what you do. It reflects Melchester Rovers. It reflects on your family. And, most of all, it reflects on you and who you are.

This was another lesson. Another chance to learn. Roy knew that. The video Sam Bustard took at college. Now this. Roy looked into his mum's eyes and made it clear to her that he'd got the message. He saw her smile.

Now, he thought, it's time for the Villa match. The one we have to win.

ROY COULDN'T STOP himself grinning as he walked on the pitch for the home match against Weston Villa. This was his first start at Mel Park. This was how his dream had always played out. Him walking on the pitch.

And to add to that Roy received a special cheer from the crowd as he was photographed being given his first pair of Gola boots.

The dream was coming true. Roy was still grinning about it when the two teams' players shook hands. The giant Weston Villa central defender – David Hartley – glared at him.

'You can wipe that smile off your face, kid,' he growled as he put out his hand. 'You're going to have a rough ride today.'

Roy took the hand of the central defender and felt his being crushed. Roy stared back at the man and tried to keep smiling. The first thing was to show he was not bothered.

From early on in the game it looked like the defender was wrong. Roy got lots of touches of the ball. He was working nicely with the three forwards around him: Pat Nolan, Vic Guthrie and Paco Diaz. It felt like they had just picked up from where they'd left off at Tynecaster and the training match against Prestwich. And Roy could sense that the passing and moving they'd been working on in training was doing the team good. The other team was all power and bullying, like Coach had said. But, because Melchester's touch and control was bang on, they were negating the physical advantage Villa had over them.

Twenty minutes in, Roy took the ball with his back to goal – Hartley behind him, all but knocking him off the ball. Roy laid the ball off to Nolan, then headed to the penalty area, not quite hurdling the outstretched leg of Hartley. Roy stumbled, but was on his feet to see Nolan fire the ball into the box for Vic Guthrie to head into the roof of the net.

GOAL!

Cue celebrations.

Roy sprinted half the length of the pitch to Guthrie and jumped on his back.

'Not bad for a midfielder!' Roy shouted to a laughing Guthrie.

Melchester Rovers 1-0 Weston Villa.

And now the hope, the dream, the chance of three points.

In the second half, Villa were committing

more to attack, looking more and more likely to equalise. But their next attack broke down, Lofty Peak winning it in the middle of the field. Lofty looked up and fired a long ball to Paco Diaz.

One outrageous flick from Diaz lofted the ball into the path of Roy's marauding run. Roy drove his right foot into the turf and hit the ball hard with his left.

The rocket.

Weston Villa's keeper reached out and arched his back, but he wasn't getting near it. The ball hit the underside of the bar, the thumping sound followed by a crescendo of cheers and shouting from the Melchester faithful.

Melchester Rovers 2-0 Weston Villa.

Now Guthrie was on Roy's back, his shouting deafening Roy.

'THAT is how you do it, Guthrie,' Roy

screamed as they fell on the turf. 'Proper goal, that!'

Guthrie laughed. 'You're getting a bit cocky, Race! But keep scoring and I can live with it.'

Neither Vic nor Roy saw David Hartley, the Villa defender, looking over at them, his face red, his eyes redder. With rage.

Ten minutes left. Still 2-0 to Melchester.

Roy heard Johnny Dexter barking out orders.

'Play deeper... Take no risks... Keep possession.'

Villa were still pressing for a goal. And, if they scored, 2-1 with ten minutes to go would be tricky to defend. Which is why Roy gave it everything when he saw Paco Diaz free on the right again. Losing his marker with a burst of pace, Roy sprinted to the edge of the area as Diaz squared the ball for him.

Roy slowed, took control of the ball with his first touch, drawing the keeper to the edge of the area. Then he dinked the ball over him as he dropped to block the ball, skirted round him and smiled as he faced a wide open goal. No keeper. No defender. Just Roy, the ball, the goal.

Roy just couldn't believe it. But he knew a tackle from the aggressive defender would be coming in soon. He rolled the ball towards the goal.

'Second one today!' he said to himself.

A sudden shout. Roy heard it like he always heard Johnny Dexter.

'LOOK OUT, RACE!'

Then Roy was up in the air, a pain in the back of his legs as he fell back to the pitch.

He heard the Melchester fans celebrating. The ball must have gone in. A noise like that. Then very quickly, silence, cheers dying down. Roy was confused, but because he knew this stadium better than any other, he also knew something bad had happened.

It was only now that he realised that the bad thing had happened to him.

And, as he lay there, pain shooting up his legs and spine like fire, all he could think of was his mum's words when she'd been putting him right earlier in the week.

It could happen in training, it could happen at Mel Park... any player, sixteen or thirty-six, could take a career-ending injury any day of the week.

Teamwork Teams

THIS BOOK IS as much about Roy's family being a team as it is about Roy's on the pitch team, Melchester Rovers. Just as Roy is part of a strong family team with his mum and dad and Rocky, so am I. My wife and daughter do so much to help me make my books and writing career as good as I can. Thank you to them!

Speaking of teamwork, a huge thank you to the Roy of the Rovers team at Rebellion: Rob Power, Rob Williams, Lisa Henke, Ben Willsher and Keith Richardson.

A big thank you to two book experts – Emma Hughes and Maryanne Proctor – who are part of the Nazeing Book Club in Essex and who read the early draft of *Teamwork* and gave me some really helpful and intelligent feedback.

Thank you – as always – to my Roy of the Rovers consultant and friend, Simon Robinson. And finally, thank you to Marcelo Bielsa.

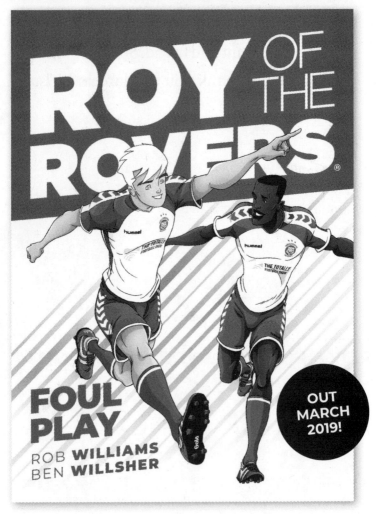

ROY OF THE ROVERS GOES DIGITAL!

Roy of the Rovers is back, with brand new comics and books starring Roy Race and the mighty Melchester Rovers – and now you can keep up to date with all things Roy on your smartphone or tablet!

Through the new *Roy of the Rovers* app, you'll be able to read the awesome new stories, grab some free comics, and even play Rovers-themed word games!

SEARCH FOR *ROY OF THE ROVERS* IN YOUR APP STORE OF CHOICE!

ROY OF THE ROVERS®
THE FIRST SEASON

Keep track of every new *Roy of the Rovers* book here!
Don't forget to tick the boxes as you read each one.

FICTION

BOOK 1	BOOK 2	BOOK 3
SCOUTED	**TEAMWORK**	**PLAYOFFS**
Author: Tom Palmer	Author: Tom Palmer	Author: Tom Palmer
Out: October 2018	Out: February 2019	Out: May 2019
ISBN: 978-1-78108-698-8	ISBN: 978-1-78108-707-7	ISBN: 978-1-78108-722-0
Roy Race is the most talented striker in Melchester – but is he good enough to catch the eye of the Melchester Rovers scouts?	Life gets tricky for Roy as he adjusts to life in the spotlight. Fortune and glory await, but can Roy juggle football, fame and family?	Crunch time for Rovers: the end of the season is here, the club is in deep trouble, and it's down to Roy to bring a bit of hope back to the Melchester faithful.
READ? ☐	**READ?** ☐	**READ?** ☐

COMICS

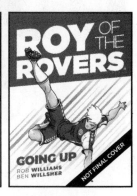

BOOK 1
KICK-OFF

Writer: Rob Williams
Artist: Ben Willsher
Out: November 2018
ISBN: 978-1-78108-652-0

Roy Race is 16, talented, and desperate to make it as a footballer. But is he good enough for Melchester Rovers? Now's the time to prove if he's got what it takes to become Roy of the Rovers.

READ? ☐

BOOK 2
FOUL PLAY

Writer: Rob Williams
Artist: Ben Willsher
Out: March 2019
ISBN: 978-1-78108-669-8

Roy picks up an injury that puts him on the sidelines, and suddenly there's competition for his place as a brand new - and brilliant - striker is brought in by the management...

READ? ☐

BOOK 3
GOING UP

Writer: Rob Williams
Artist: Ben Willsher
Out: June 2019
ISBN: 978-1-78108-673-5

Roy and the team have battled through a tough season, but have they got enough left to get promoted? Or will they fall at the final hurdle and see the club sold by its greedy owner?

READ? ☐